✔ KU-515-106

USBORNE HOTSHOTS
BEADS &
BANGLES

USBORNE HOTSHOTS
BEADS &
BANGLES

Ray Gibson

Edited by Cheryl Evans and Nicole Irving
Designed by Helen Westwood and Vicki Groombridge

Illustrated by Jonathan Woodcock
Photographs by Howard Allman

Series editor: Judy Tatchell
Series designer: Ruth Russell

CONTENTS

Getting started

This book shows you how to make all sorts of beads and bracelets from low-cost materials and how to turn beads into lovely things to wear. Here are some skills and techniques that will help you.

Threading beads

Usually, you thread beads onto a needle with a double thread. You can also thread them onto some of the things shown below.

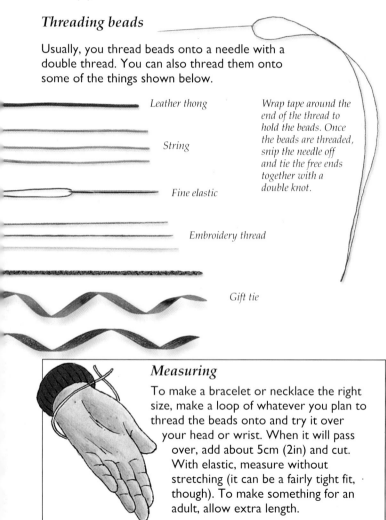

Leather thong

String

Fine elastic

Embroidery thread

Gift tie

Wrap tape around the end of the thread to hold the beads. Once the beads are threaded, snip the needle off and tie the free ends together with a double knot.

Measuring

To make a bracelet or necklace the right size, make a loop of whatever you plan to thread the beads onto and try it over your head or wrist. When it will pass over, add about 5cm (2in) and cut. With elastic, measure without stretching (it can be a fairly tight fit, though). To make something for an adult, allow extra length.

4

Making a bead stand

A bead stand is a useful thing to have. See how to make it here.

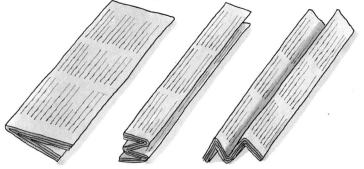

1. Cut four layers of newspaper into a long strip 12cm (5in) wide. Fold the strip in two, bringing the long sides together.

2. Fold each half down to meet the middle fold. Place this stand on a tray if you think you will want to move it around.

Using the bead stand

Measure how long you want your necklace or bracelet to be (see left). Make a stand that is longer, and mark the exact length on it. Fill the stand until you reach the mark, then you have enough beads.

Arrange the beads in size or pattern order on your stand. Thread them, starting from one end and working to the other.

Paper beads

You will need:

- bright wrapping paper about 52 x 68cm (20 x 25in)
- 3¾mm knitting needle (US size 4)
- big paintbrush
- household glue (PVA) mixed with a little water*
- petroleum jelly
- ruler

Tapered beads

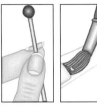

1. Cut a strip of bright paper 2 x 68cm (¾ x 25in). Starting from the middle, taper both edges to a point at one end.

2. Coat the knitting needle with a thin layer of petroleum jelly. Carefully brush the glue and water mix thinly over the back of the strip.

The three threads of this necklace are strung through two beads at each end, then tied to either side of a screw clasp (from a craft store).

Make each row of beads shorter than the last. You need about fifty beads.

*Use the glue for gluing and varnishing – see page 15.

3. Roll the strip around the knitting needle a few times to form a central hole. Slip the bead off the needle and keep on rolling.

Balance needle on food cans.

4. Guide the strip so it stays central on the bead. Thread the bead onto a knitting needle to dry. If you like, varnish it with glue and water mix.

Beads threaded onto a leather thong can be tied as a bracelet or a necklace.

Add beads on the loose ends between two knots.

Here you can see what a huge variety of paper beads you can make.

Use thick paper to make fatter beads.

Start with wider or narrower strips to make bigger or smaller beads.

Straight beads

To make straight beads, cut straight strips of paper 1 x 68cm (½ x 25in). Paste, roll up and varnish in the same way as for tapered beads.

Piggy necklace

You will need:

- silver florists' wire (from a florist's)
- baking tray
- kitchen foil
- craft knife and scissors
- pink, green and red oven-hardening clay
- large needle
- three toothpicks
- fine elastic
- clear tape

You need to make 4 pigs and about 40 apple beads. Put four apple beads between each pig.

Pig beads

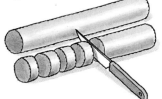

The loop must be at this angle.

1. Soften some pink clay in your hands and roll into a sausage shape. Cut this into pea-sized pieces. Roll them into balls.

2. Cover upturned baking tray with foil. Put a clay ball near its edge, press it and put a wire loop (see right) in the middle.

3. Flatten another ball a little more than the first, to make it larger. Press it over the first, covering the wire stem.

4. Roll two small pear shapes for ears and press on. Add a small round snout. Mark eyes and nostrils with a toothpick.

Making wire loops

For each pig you need a loop made like this:

 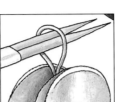 

Trim the loop's tail to 1½cm (¾in).

1. Tape together two toothpicks. Loop a piece of wire about 9cm (4in) long around them.

2. Bring the wire together under the sticks and hold it firmly. Keep holding it during step 3.

3. Twist the sticks around three or four times. The wire winds around itself, leaving a loop. Slip the loop off.

Apple beads

To make equal-sized beads, cut a clay sausage in half, then each piece in half again and again until they are the size you want.

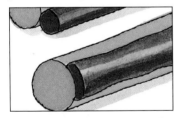 

1. Soften some green clay and roll it into a sausage shape. Add a fine strip of softened red clay to the side. Gently roll them both together.

2. For each bead, cut a pea-sized piece of clay and roll it into a ball. Put it on the upturned tray. Pierce all the way through it carefully with a toothpick.

Baking and threading

Bake at 140°C / 275°F / gas mark 1 for 10 to 15 minutes, or follow what the package says. Ask an adult to help.

Once the clay is cold, thread the beads on enough elastic for a necklace (see page 4). Tie with a double knot.

9

Metal heart pendants

You will need:

- two small pieces of cardboard
- small hammer and a nail
- flat piece of wood
- 6 x 6cm (2½ x 2½in) piece of tracing paper
- clear tape
- rag
- pencil
- glue stick
- old gloves
- old scissors
- sandpaper
- clean, empty soft drink can

○ *Hole for threading*

Use this outline as a template for the heart.

1. Tape the can firmly to a flat surface. Ask an adult to pierce a hole in the can with the scissors. Remove the tape.

2. Put on the gloves. Push the point of the scissors into the hole. Cut a square about 6 x 6cm (2½ x 2½in).

Trim the trace to the square.

3. Flatten the metal square by bending it back and then rubbing it firmly all over with the rag on a flat surface.

4. Trace the heart template at the top of the page and mark the hole. Glue the trace to the metal square's plain side.

5. Tape the square to the piece of wood. Use the nail to press a dent in the metal where the hole mark is.

10

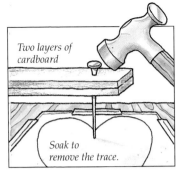

Two layers of cardboard

Soak to remove the trace.

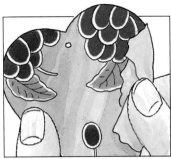

6. Push the nail through the cardboard. Hold this and place the nail in the dent. Tap the nail through the metal.

7. Cut out the heart. Sandpaper the edges and around the hole on the other side. Thread onto the middle of a leather thong.

Jewel heart

Follow steps 1-7 to make a big heart, plain side up (put the trace on the patterned side).

You also need:
- kitchen foil
- bright foil wrapper

1. Crumple some foil. Wrap it in the bright wrapper. Press this jewel on a flat surface.

2. Glue the jewel to the middle of the heart. Glue a strip of folded foil around it.

Knot thong around hole, then tie around neck for a pendant.

For a brooch like this, take a thread through a bow, two beads, a pendant, and back the same way. Sew a safety pin to the back of the bow.

Big bold beads

You will need:

- kitchen foil
- ruler
- scissors
- old gloves
- fine elastic
- large needle (for tapestry or darning)
- a bead stand (see page 5) on a tray

1. For a large middle bead cut a square of foil 20 x 20cm (8 x 8in). Crumple this into a ball.

Make the foil ball as round as possible.

2. Put on the gloves. Roll the ball firmly between the palms of your hands. Place it in the middle of the bead stand.

3. Make two smaller foil balls from 18cm (7in) squares, then two each from 16, 14 and 12cm squares (6, 5 and 4in).

Put the biggest bead in the middle.

4. Put the foil balls on the stand, placing one of each size on either side so they are in size order, from big to small.

To thread, pierce the balls with a needle threaded with elastic.

5. Make foil balls from 10cm (3in) squares to add to both ends to make the length you need (see page 4).

12

Papier mâché beads

Make foil balls as shown opposite.

You also need:
- *papier mâché pulp (see right)*
- *acrylic paints*
- *paintbrush*

1. Roll a ball of *papier mâché* pulp about the size of a foil bead. Flatten it into a circle and wrap it around the bead.

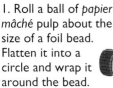

2. Roll the ball in your palms and leave to dry on the stand. Once dry, pierce each one with a needle. Paint white, dry, then decorate.

Making papier mâché

Cut layers of newspaper into 1½cm (½in) squares. Soak for three hours in hot water, then squeeze and mash with your fingers into a pulp. Put the pulp into a mesh strainer and press out most of the water. In a bowl, mix a tablespoon of household glue (PVA) into the pulp. Add more glue and mix together until the pulp feels like squishy clay.

Silver foil beads

Papier mâché beads

These beads are big, but light to wear.

These silver foil beads are rolled in a little paint in your palms, so the silver still shines through.

13

Birthday card beads

These beads are a really good way to recycle cards you have been sent — they are a good souvenir of a very special card you want to remember, too. You could use cards with seasonal pictures on them to make Christmas or Easter earrings.

Card beads look good threaded with paper beads (see pages 6-7).

1. Choose a part of the card you particularly like. Place the jar on it, draw around it and cut out the circle.

String the loops of the beads onto thread for a necklace. Put other beads in between to separate them, and around the back.

The card beads will stay flat on your neck when you put the necklace on.

For each bead you will need:

- a wire loop*
- a small bead
- clear tape
- a greeting card
- pencil
- scissors
- small round jar
- glue stick
- darning needle

*Make as shown on page 9, but loop the wire around one toothpick and leave a long tail.

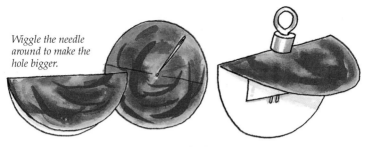

Wiggle the needle around to make the hole bigger.

2. Fold the circle in half. Press along the fold, then open it out. Push the needle into the middle of the fold line.

3. Thread the wire loop through the bead, then through the hole made with the needle in the circle. Tape the tail down.

4. Glue the two sides together and allow to dry. Twist the loop, so it lies at right angles to the bead, ready for threading.

Thread several card beads on the front of the necklace.

Small card beads

For smaller card beads, start with a half circle. Fold it in two, tape a wire loop inside, then glue the two sides together.

Use smaller beads in between the card beads and around the back of the necklace.

Varnishing

If the card you use is not shiny, you can varnish it. Paint the finished beads with household glue (PVA) mixed in a mug with a little water. The mixture looks white at first, but dries clear. Allow the varnish to dry and apply more coats, if you like.

15

Bright felt beads

Felt comes in amazing bright shades that you can mix and match.

Rolled felt beads

For each bead you need:

- a felt square
- graph paper
- toothpick
- ruler
- pencil
- scissors
- glue stick
- pins

1. Draw a strip 1cm (½in) wide on the graph paper. Cut it out, then pin it to the felt and cut along its edge.

2. Take off the paper. Roll the felt strip tightly around the toothpick until the bead is the size you want. Trim the edge.

Felt is light and soft to wear.

This necklace is made of bound felt beads (see opposite). Thread eight beads on a few strands of embroidery thread. For a bracelet, thread six beads on enough fine elastic to go over your hand (see page 4).

Stripy rolls

Make rolled beads from two contrasting strips of felt. Roll them together around a toothpick. Glue the inner loose end down, then the outer one.

3. Holding the felt firmly, gently pull the toothpick out. Glue the loose end down securely and leave to dry.

To make beads with a two-tone effect, roll a strip of felt, glue, then roll another shade on top and glue. For rolled felt beads, push the needle through the sides of the beads to thread them.

Bound felt beads

Small, glass beads don't cost much and you can sew some directly onto your felt beads.

1. Glue one side of a strip of felt and wrap around a straw. Trim the straw at each end.

2. Bind each bead with yarn and threads. Tie these securely. Trim the ends neatly.

You will need:

- felt squares
- plastic straws
- glue stick
- embroidery threads
- knitting yarns
- gold or silver thread
- tiny glass beads
- scissors

Slip a few glass beads on the thread as you wind.

17

New bangles for old

Here are some ideas for decorating old bangles. You could also buy bangles that don't cost much especially to decorate them.

Painting a plastic bangle

Paint doesn't stay well on plastic, so it's best to cover a plastic bangle with paper first.

1. Tear newspaper into 1½cm (¾in) squares. Mix together equal amounts of glue and water.

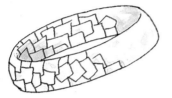

2. Dip the squares in the mixture and cover both sides of the bangle with them. Overlap the pieces.

3. Paint the bangle white and leave to dry. Decorate with patterns, then varnish with glue and water mixed (see page 15).

Découpage

Découpage is a French word meaning cutting out. Paint a bangle all over. Cut out small shapes from bright gift wrap. Glue them onto the bangle, then add varnish (see page 15).

Glitzy bangle

1. Take any bangle. Dab paint onto a piece of foil. Leave to dry, then cut the foil into 1½cm (¾in) strips.

2. Glue one end of a strip to a bangle, wind it around and glue the other end. Add more strips, overlapping them as you go.

3. Neatly cover the bangle with short pieces of clear tape. Then smooth it all over by polishing with a soft cloth.

Painting a wooden bangle

Rub the bangle with fine sandpaper, then paint it white and leave to dry. Decorate with paint as you like.

Fancy fish necklace

For a fish bead you need:

- large, clear plastic soft drink bottle
- craft knife
- tracing paper
- plastic straw
- scissors
- clear tape
- pencil
- glue stick
- thin cardboard
- acrylic paints
- paintbrush
- waterproof felt-tip pen

Use this outline for your fish template.

1. Make a hole with the craft knife at one end of the bottle. Push the scissors in and cut around it. Repeat at other end.

2. Cut all the way up the tube in a straight line. Then wash the piece of plastic thoroughly and dry it well with a cloth.

3. Trace the fish template above. Glue the trace onto the cardboard. Once the glue is dry, cut out the fish shape.

The fish will lie flat against your neck when you wear the necklace.

Arch

Paint the underside of the curved plastic.

4. Lay the plastic so that it arches off the table. Using the cut-out shape, draw fish outlines on the plastic with the felt-tip pen.

5. Cut the fish out, just outside the pen line. Use bright paints to pattern them with scales, stripes and spots. Paint an eye.

6. Leave to dry, then paint in a background over the patterns. Both of these will show through on the other side of the plastic shape.

Overlap the tape a little.

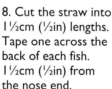

The straw goes on the taped side.

Stringing the fish

To string the fish, push fine elastic through the pieces of straw. Combine with other types of beads, if you like.

7. When the paint is dry, cover the painted side with strips of clear tape. Trim the edges all around the shape.

8. Cut the straw into 1½cm (½in) lengths. Tape one across the back of each fish. 1½cm (½in) from the nose end.

Silky bangles

Silky embroidery threads make these
brilliant bangles really eye-catching.

You will need:

- about 25cm
  (10in) of plastic
  tubing from a
  pet shop (this
  is sold for use in
  fish tanks and
  is not expensive)
- scissors
- six-stranded
  embroidery silk
- clear tape
- craft knife
- needle with a
  large eye

1. Cut a piece of
tubing long enough to
make a circle that will
pass over your hand.

*Here, metallic yarn is
passed through a few
glass beads to add extra
interest to the bangle.*

*You can buy a
huge range of
embroidery
threads.*

*Here is a
different idea for a
bangle made from
plastic tubing – see
page 25 for how
to do it.*

*Use different shades
to cover all the bangle.*

*These bangles look stunning if you
choose threads to match a special
outfit and wear them together.*

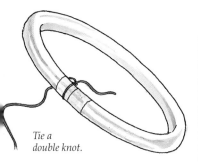

Tie a double knot.

2. Stick the two ends of the tubing together with clear tape. Tie a thread around the tubing.

3. Trim the short end of the thread to about 2cm (¾in), then tape it down onto the tubing as shown above.

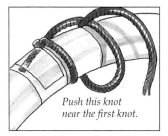

Push this knot near the first knot.

4. Bring the long end of the thread around the tube, then pass it back through itself, making a knot.

5. Make lots of knots in this way. Keep them all lined up neatly and pushed up close together.

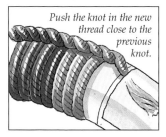

Push the knot in the new thread close to the previous knot.

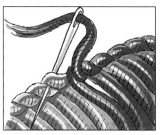

6. Trim and tape the thread end. Now start with a new thread, following steps 2-5.

7. To finish, thread the free end on a needle. Sew it firmly into the first knot, then trim.

Fringed and glitter bangles

Here are some more bangles to make using the versatile plastic tubing described on page 22.

Fringed bangles

You will need:

- bangle made as in steps 1-2 on page 22
- knitting yarn
- clear tape
- craft knife
- scissors
- 8cm (3in) wide strip of cardboard

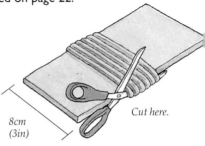

8cm (3in)

Cut here.

1. Wind some yarn six times around the cardboard. Cut at the bottom to make a six-stranded loop.

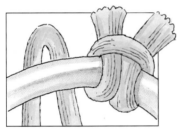

2. Place the loop as shown. Take the ends around the bangle, up through the loop, then pull them tight.

3. Add fringed loops like this all the way around. To finish, trim all the fringes to the length you want.

These graded shades of yellow and red make a bright, glowing fringed bangle.

Other ideas

You can fill the tubes with all kinds of tiny things for different effects. Try tiny cake decorations or small seeds such as poppy and sesame.

Fringed bangles are chunky and look great with sweaters.

Glitter bangles often look good worn in twos or threes.

If you like, you can hide the clear tape by binding some thread over it.

This bangle is filled with tiny cake decorations.

Glitter bangles

Stick a piece of clear tape over one end of a piece of plastic tubing. Pour glitter into your hand.

Tape over the end.

Scoop the glitter into the tube until it is full. Block the other end with tape, then tape the two ends together.

Pom pom beads

You will need:

- double knitting yarn
- crochet hook
- tracing paper
- sharp scissors
- pencil
- darning needle
- cardboard at least 4 x 8cm (1½ x 3in)

Fold the cardboard in half with the short sides together.

Cut out two cardboard rings.

1. Trace the circles template below onto the folded cardboard. Cut out the big circle through both layers. Cut out the inner circles to make two rings.

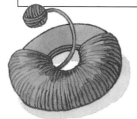

Thread yarn onto a darning needle to wind when hole gets small.

Tie with yarn 75cm (30in) long.

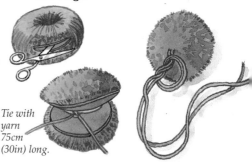

2. Wind the yarn into a ball that fits through the hole. Tie the end around both rings together and wind the yarn around and around.

3. When the hole is full, snip around the yarn between the two rings. Part the rings and tie yarn tightly around the middle.

4. Tear off the card rings and fluff out the pom pom. Tie a loose knot in the yarn ends, as close to the pom pom as you can.

Circles template

Place tracing paper over the circles. Trace them off in pencil. Scribble over the lines with a soft pencil. Turn the trace over, place on the cardboard and go over the lines with a hard pencil.

Leave ends
18cm (7in) long.

Pull hard to
tighten.

5. Put the crochet hook through the knot. Hold the hook and pom pom in your right hand and the yarn in your left.

6. With the knot in your left hand, catch a loop of double yarn with the crochet hook. Pull it through the loop of the knot.

7. Keep hooking yarn through the previous loop until the chain is as long as you want. Then pull the yarn through the end loop.

Brooch

Stitch the yarn ends over the fixed side of a big safety pin or kilt pin. Stitch for another 1cm (½in). Take the needle back through the stitches and sew neatly into the top of the chain, then cut.

Earrings

For a two-tone pom pom, wind with one shade, then change to another.

Thread the yarn ends of two pom poms onto a needle and sew them into the tops of the chains. Poke a kidney wire (see page 30) through the joined chains.

Earrings and brooches

You can use any of the beads in this book to make projects of your own. Here are some ways to use beads to make brooches and earrings.

Brooches

Glue suitable beads onto a small piece of cardboard. Glue a brooch back onto the other side (or tape on the fixed side of a safety pin – see page 30).

For a brooch like this, cut cardboard the size you want. Paint or cover it with pretty paper. Glue the beads on.

How to make bead earrings

1. Cut a piece of silver florists' wire as long as the bead. Bend it in half.

Attach these earrings to clip or pierced earring findings that have a loop.

Push glue in with a toothpick.

2. Put some household glue (PVA) into the top of the bead.

3. Loop the wire through a pierced earring finding (see page 30).

4. Gently push the two wire ends into the glued end of the bead. Leave to dry.

28

Paper bead long earrings

You will need:

- six tapered and two straight paper beads (page 6)
- four round beads about 1cm (½in) across – buy these
- two 30cm (12in) lengths of florists' silver wire or fuse wire
- a pair of kidney wire findings (see page 30)

1. Thread a round bead, then a tapered bead, to halfway along one wire. Take one end back through the tapered bead.

2. Thread another tapered bead and a round one. Double the wire back through the tapered bead. Twist the wire ends together.

3. Thread the wires through a tapered and a straight bead. Slip one wire end through the loop in the kidney wire and bend back down.

4. Twist the other end around the bent wire. Dab glue on the ends and push back into the bead. Make another earring the same.

For clip earrings, you could glue small paper or felt beads to squares of cardboard, then onto earring clip findings (see page 30).

Make earrings from beads with a loop, such as the pig beads on pages 8-9, by pushing an earring attachment through the loop.

Tips and information

Here are some more tips and ideas for making your own beads projects look as professional and interesting as possible.

Long glass beads

Tiny glass beads come in all shapes and sizes.

Buying beads

Beads are expensive to buy, which is what makes creating your own so worthwhile. When you make something, though, think of mixing them with just a few beads from an old or broken necklace, or just a few choice beads from a craft supplier.

Tiny glass beads are not expensive and look good mixed with handmade beads. They can also be used to decorate bigger beads or bangles (such as the felt beads on page 16 and the silky bangles on page 22). Look out for mixed packets of beads being sold cheaply.

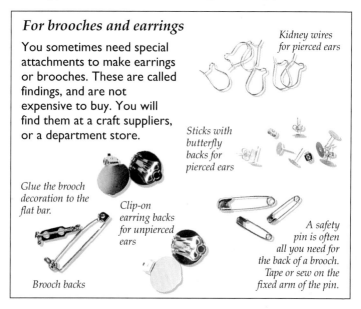

For brooches and earrings

You sometimes need special attachments to make earrings or brooches. These are called findings, and are not expensive to buy. You will find them at a craft suppliers, or a department store.

Kidney wires for pierced ears

Sticks with butterfly backs for pierced ears

Glue the brooch decoration to the flat bar.

Clip-on earring backs for unpierced ears

A safety pin is often all you need for the back of a brooch. Tape or sew on the fixed arm of the pin.

Brooch backs

Going further

Experiment by changing the size, shape and style of any beads to make your own, unique items. Here are some alternatives to the paper beads on pages 6-7, for example.

Use gold or silver paper for these beads.

Small beads: make straight beads, only with narrower strips. You can roll them around a toothpick for a smaller hole.

Long beads: make tapered beads, but start with strips with a wide end of 4 or 5cm (1½ or 2in).

Newspaper beads: make long beads (see above) out of newspaper. Paint them with acrylic paints.

Tips

For the best results when making beads, always work on a clean table and keep your hands clean.

Save scraps to use in your projects. Foil wrappers, gift wrap, gift tie, threads, fabric and old necklaces will all come in handy.

Varnishing tip

If you varnish any of your beads (those on page 15, for example), here's a way to do it without getting in a mess.

Thread single beads onto toothpicks. Stick these in half a clean, dry, raw potato. Carefully paint the varnish on from top to bottom, then leave to dry.

Use the potato a little like a pincushion for the toothpicks.

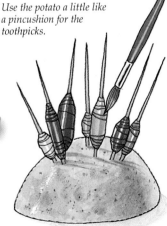

Index

Additional editorial: Flic Everett and Carol Garbera
Additional design by Robert Walster and Camilla Luff
Illustrations pages 26-27 by Lily Whitlock; pages 6-7 by Prue Greener
Photograph page 27 by Simon Bottomley

This book is based on material previously published in *The Usborne Book of Beads, Bangles and Bracelets*, *The Usborne Book of Making Presents* and *The Usborne Book of Jewellery*.

First published in 1996 by Usborne Publishing Ltd, Usborne House, 83-85 Saffron Hill, London EC1N 8RT, England.

Copyright © 1996, 1995, 1990, 1987 Usborne Publishing Ltd.

The name Usborne and the device 🎈 are Trade Marks of Usborne Publishing Ltd. All rights reserved. No part of this publication may be reproduced, stored in a retrieval system or transmitted in any form or by any means, electronic, mechanical, photocopying, recording or otherwise, without the prior permission of the publisher. First published in America August 1996. UE. Printed in Italy.